Life According to Dani

WRITTEN BY

Rose Lagercrantz

ILLUSTRATED BY

Eva Eriksson

GECKO PRESS

CONTENTS

Chapter 1

It is summer break—Dani's first! Dani who lives
in the yellow house on Home Street. But she hasn't
been there for a long time.

Last time was just before school finished for the year.

When she left home that morning it was raining,
and worms were squirming on the road where they
could get run over.

So Dani picked them up and moved them out
of the way.

That day she saved the lives of nine worms and four snails.

But only a couple of hours later an unbelievable thing happened: her own father was run over.

Why hadn't someone turned up to save him? Why didn't the driver toot or something?

He was all right, but he has to stay in the hospital for several months.

Dani ended up spending the summer break with Ella, her best friend in the world. She went with her to an island in the sea.

On the island they played all day long and built
huts and fished and swam.

They spend all their time playing when they get
together. It starts as soon as they see each other.

They were having so much fun on the island that
Dani hardly had time to miss her father. They went
swimming five, six, or seven times a day.

Their swimsuits were always wet and having
to be hung on the washing line.

Sometimes they didn't bother with swimsuits
and went skinny-dipping.

Like the water sprite in old stories, who sits naked on a stone playing the violin.

Anyone who hears him goes a bit crazy and starts dancing.

Ella also plays the violin.

Her mother usually makes her work on her pieces half an hour a day, but how could she when Dani was there and they had so many games to play! Playing was their most important thing.

They watched wild animals too—like the fox that sat on the cliff sometimes, looking out to sea.

Or they spied on the moose swimming
through the water.

Sometimes eagles circled over
the island—sea eagles.
  As soon as they got close,
the other birds started
to shriek.

Their wings were enormous. And their claws!

If an eagle turned up, they ran with Roy and Partyboy into the house. They're Ella's hamsters.

It was only when Dani thought about her own hamsters that she got homesick. She missed Snow and Flake.

The poor things weren't allowed to come, and had to stay with Grandma and Grandpa.

Otherwise the whole island would soon be full of hamsters, Ella's mother said, because they were bound to have babies.

Roy and Partyboy happen to be boys and Snow and Flake are girls.

Sometimes Dani missed her cat too.

A little.

But most of all she missed her dad.

Every evening he called Dani and asked what she'd been up to.

As soon as they'd talked to each other
Dani felt better.

Chapter 2

But one morning when Dani woke up she remembered that her father hadn't called her the night before.

She was very worried.

Ella was fast asleep. When Dani poked her she just smiled and turned over.

And Miranda, Ella's little sister, who slept in the same room, was in with her grandmother.

So there was no one to talk to.

Dani tiptoed into the kitchen, where Ella's mother and her extra father Paddy sat drinking coffee.

"You're awake early," said Paddy.

"You look a bit worried," said Ella's mother.

"Yes, I think something's happened to my dad again," said Dani.

"Why do you think that?" asked Paddy.

"He didn't call yesterday."

"He was probably busy." Ella's mother made Dani a salami sandwich.

Paddy poured her a glass of milk.

But Dani was so worried she couldn't eat or drink a thing.

Luckily, it wasn't long before Ella woke up and came into the kitchen.

She understood immediately that something was the matter.

"What is it?" she asked.

Dani swallowed.

Ella sat down at the table and looked at her.

"Dani's a little worried," said Ella's mother.

Dani sniffed.

"My dad didn't call yesterday!"

"That is strange," Ella agreed.

"He'll be in touch soon." Paddy was sure. "Why don't you go out and see if you can find the fox?"

"Not today," said Ella. "Today we'll do something different. I know! Let's make a BAKING BOOK! Shall we, Dani?"

And soon they were under way.

They began with a recipe for coconut peaks.

Ella wrote down how to do it.

Buy a packet of dried coconut and
do what it says on the back.

Dani drew the pictures. She drew coconut peaks
that looked like small knobbly mountains and she
filled them in with a yellow crayon.

Then Ella added a little brown.

They looked good.

The first page in their baking book was good.

But suddenly a dark shadow fell on Dani.
She had thought about her father again.

"If only I knew why he didn't call," she sighed, looking out the window.

Ella followed her gaze anxiously.

Far away on the water a lone ferry was coming towards the jetty.

Ella pushed away the paper and crayons.

"Look, Dani, the boat's coming! And we haven't even started the basket!"

Every morning at nine, Dani and Ella prepared a basket with coffee, juice, and buns. Then they ran with it down to the jetty.

At ten past nine the boat pulled in and stayed only a few minutes, so you had to be there on time if you wanted to do business.

And they did. Selling to the passengers was their summer job, said Ella.

Chapter 3

This morning they arrived at the very last minute.
The boat was just coming in.

"Coffee, juice, and buns!" yelled Ella when the passengers came ashore.

"Extra cheap today!" Dani shouted, even though it cost the same every day. It was a business trick.

Soon they were flat out making sales.

By the time the boat left, there was nothing in their basket.

Except for silver and gold coins and even a twenty-dollar note!

Ella counted how much they had.

"We're stinking rich!" she said happily.

"What shall we do with all the money?" asked Dani.

"I thought we might go to Iceland and ride Iceland ponies," said Ella.

"You've never told me that!"

"I thought about it last night while you were asleep. Good idea, don't you think?"

Dani didn't answer. She's a bit scared of horses. They can kick.

But at that moment there was nothing to worry about. She was thinking what a great summer job they had!

Chapter 4

Somebody not so excited about their business was Ella's mother.

She was the one who made the coffee and baked the buns.

She has to bake all the time. On the island there's no bakery where you can buy bread and buns and cakes.

When they came back from the jetty she was busy making coconut peaks.

"Aha, so you sneaked a look at our baking book," said Ella.

"No," said her mother. "I didn't need to. I know how to make them."

"Can I taste?"

"No, you'll have to wait."

"Wait for what?"

"I'm not telling! It's a surprise."

Ella went into a sulk. She can get like that sometimes. Really sulky. And it takes a while to blow over.

But her mother pretended not to notice.

"Now, Ella, you can take your violin down to the boathouse and play your pieces again," she said tartly.

Ella sighed all the way to the cupboard where her violin lives on a special shelf.

Only she and her mother are allowed to touch it because it's so special.

"What will Dani be doing?" she asked.

"Dani can pick up all the things you've been throwing around. It'll be nice and tidy in here!"

"What good is that?" muttered Ella.

But she took the violin case and trudged off to the boathouse.

And Dani picked up all the soft toys, books,
crayons, pens, cards, and clothes that were scattered
all over the floor, and threw them into a cupboard.

Then she ran down to the boathouse too.

From quite a long way off she could hear the wail
of the violin.

Dani knocked hard on the door and peeped in
through the window. The violin went quiet and Ella
opened the door.

"You took ages tidying up," she complained.

"Yes, it was hard work," said Dani.

"Come on, let's go for a swim," said Ella.

"But you're supposed to be playing your violin,"
Dani reminded her.

"I can do that too," Ella explained. "We'll pretend
I'm the water sprite!"

They hurried down to the beach and pulled off
their clothes.

Soon Ella was in the water sawing wildly at the
violin, while Dani danced around her like a crazy
thing.

She threw her head about, twirled, and yelled at
the top of her voice.

But then she stopped mid-leap. Someone was running down the beach.

Dani squinted to see in the sharp sunlight.

It was her cousin Sven! Behind Sven came
Grandma, with Ella's mother and Paddy. So this
was the surprise.

Dani sat down with a splash.

Ella was facing out to sea and didn't notice a thing. She went on playing.

"Ella!" her mother shrieked when she saw what she was doing. "Have you gone completely crazy?"

"No!" Dani hurried to answer. "Ella's the water sprite. I'm the crazy one!"

When Ella turned and saw the others, she sank into the water, too, but kept her arms up.

Only her head, the violin, and the bow could be seen.

"Come up here at once!" her mother commanded.

But Ella did the opposite. She went backwards.

Ella's mother plunged after her, not minding about
her dress getting wet.

"Ella! Stay where you are!" called Paddy.

"Only if you do what I say!" shouted Ella.
"Everyone must leave immediately!"

"Why?"

"Because otherwise it's embarrassing!
We're skinny-dipping!"

The little group backed up and headed for the house.

Sven peeked but Dani yelled: "Don't look!"

Only when everyone had gone did they hurry out of the water and dry themselves and get dressed.

Chapter 5

Soon they were sitting on the veranda drinking juice and munching on coconut peaks. Then they had cake.

Grandma had brought good news. Dani's dad would soon be leaving the hospital.

"Won't that be nice?" She smiled at Dani.

Dani looked away.

"What is it?" asked Grandma.

"My father doesn't miss me any more," said Dani.

"Nonsense," said Grandma. "Of course he does. Your dad misses you to bits!"

"Why doesn't he call then?"

"Doesn't he?" said Grandma. "That's strange."

"No, it's not," said Sven.

Grandma looked sternly at Sven and Sven was quiet.

But as soon as Grandma started talking to the others, he leaned forward.

"I know a secret," he whispered. "Something I'm not supposed to tell, according to her."

He nodded furtively at Grandma.

"Well, don't tell then," said Ella. "We're not interested in your little secrets. Are we, Dani?"

"It's not a little secret," said Sven.

"We're not even interested in your partly big secrets," interrupted Ella.

Sven pretended not to hear.

"But I can say the first letter!" he continued. "Do you want me to?"

"Only if you must," said Ella.

Sven leaned close.

"S," he said. "The secret starts with S."

Dani and Ella looked at each other.

"Shall I say another letter?"

Dani nodded hesitantly.

"A…" said Sven.

"S-A?"

"S-A-D…" Sven said.

Ella started to laugh. "You mean *wretched
and miserable*?"

"No, because then comes I and E!"

Grandma whipped around to face him.

"Sven! Have you forgotten what you promised me? You're not to say a word to Dani about that! Not a single word!"

"I haven't," Sven protested. "I've only said five letters!"

"S-A-D-I-E." Dani sounded out the letters. "Who's that?"

"Your dad's girlfriend!" whispered Sven.

Dani felt a knife in her chest.

Grandma was fuming, but Sven took no notice.

"Grandma and Grandpa have already met her," he chattered. "She's very sweet, Grandpa says. Sweet as marzipan. And she laughs all the time!"

"Laughs?" echoed Dani. "Why does she laugh?"

"Because Gianni tells such funny stories!"

That's what he's called, Dani's dad. Giovanni is his name, but he gets called Gianni.

"I thought he was sick!" said Ella sharply.

"Yeah, but you can still tell funny stories when you're sick. By the way, Grandpa says Gianni looks much better now he has a girl."

"Sorry," he said, seeing his grandmother's furious look. "I mean girlfriend. Grandma says you're supposed to say girlfriend."

That was what had happened: Dani's father had got a girlfriend. Dani felt as if the eagle had its claws into her.

As the others talked, she turned white under her suntan.

Grandma tried to reassure her: "Take no notice of what Sven says."

Ella stood up and drilled her eyes into Sven:
"You're lying!"

Sven flared up. "I'm not lying! I've never lied in my whole life!"

"Now you're lying again," said Ella.

Sven was so angry he was almost crying.

"Grandma," he shouted, "tell them it's true! You've even met Sadie!"

Just then Paddy's phone rang. Paddy's ringtone sounds like a dog barking.

"Woof! Woof!" barked the phone.

He quickly took it out of his pocket and put it to his ear.

"That's great," he said enthusiastically. "You're very welcome. I'll be at the jetty in ten minutes."

He ended the call and turned to Dani.

"That was your father. Didn't I tell you he'd call? He has permission to leave the hospital for a few days and is on his way here in a taxi boat. I'll go and meet him with the motorbike."

"Come on, let's run to the lookout and wave," said Ella, rushing off.

Sven ran after her, but Dani sat still and stared at a fly buzzing round the empty cake plate.

She had been right after all. This was exactly what she'd sensed all morning. Something terrible had happened.

Soon Ella and Sven were back.

"He's coming!" shouted Sven. "Now you can see for yourselves if I was lying!"

"That's just what we were thinking," said Ella. "Isn't it, Dani?"

She stopped talking and looked at Dani, who sat as if she was paralyzed.

"And if what Sven says is true then we'll talk some sense into your father. Won't we, Dani?"

"What would you say to him?" Sven wondered.

"Never you mind," said Ella. "I'll take care of the talking. I'll tell him he doesn't need a girlfriend because he has one already. Both girl and friend. All in one. When you have Dani you don't need anyone else."

"And will that help?"

"Of course it will. I'll start by giving him a little welcome flower!"

Ella looked around and picked a bluebell.

"You can give him a flower too, Dani."

But Dani still sat as if she was stunned.

Chapter 6

It wasn't long before Paddy roared up with Dani's father on the bike. A woman was running up the hill behind them.

"The nurse!" cried Grandma, looking dismayed.

"Did he have to bring her along?"

At first Dani didn't understand what Grandma meant. This was a nurse?

She wasn't wearing a nurse's uniform but instead a dress covered with daisies, and she was carrying a cake box.

It looked as if they were going to have to eat another cake!

Paddy drove right up to the table and helped Gianni from the bike.

Suddenly Dani came to life.

"Dad!" she cried and rushed up and threw her arms around his neck.

"Ouch! Please, Dani, careful!" he said. "I'll fall over."

But Paddy and the flowery nurse were right there
and helped him to a chair.

Dani's father sank into it.

"There!"

He looked around and wiped his forehead.

Ella stepped forward and held out the flower.

"Welcome to our happy island," she said.

"Well, thank you!" said Dani's dad. "It's not my birthday, is it?"

"No, but you've got a girlfriend!" said Sven. "I'm not lying, am I, Gianni?"

Dani looked at her father. But he didn't seem to have heard.

"Amore!" He turned to Dani. "Come, sit here with me."

He pointed at the chair beside him.

Dani went over and sat there stiffly.

"Sit a little closer," he said, giving her a tug.

Dani inched her chair a little closer.

"You're so brown!" said Dad. "You must have been doing lots of swimming."

Dani didn't need to answer because Ella took over.

"Yes, she has. Fishing too."

"What sort of fish?" asked Dani's father.

"Perch mostly," said Ella, "but you haven't come here to talk about fish, have you, Gianni?"

"No, I haven't..."

He turned to Dani again.

He wasn't the slightest bit brown. He was white as a sheet, patched and stitched in several places.

Dani stole a glance at him.

"I know, Dani," he said, as if he could read her thoughts. "I look terrible. I shouldn't have come to see you yet, but I couldn't wait. I've missed you so terribly!"

"Why didn't you call then?" mumbled Dani.

"Haven't I called? I have! Every evening at seven o'clock after dinner!"

"No...not yesterday!"

"Come, Dani," said Dad. "Come and give me a hug."

Chapter 7

Up until now this story could have had a happy ending.

Dani's father could have had a hug and everyone would have been happy and satisfied. At least for a moment.

It was Sven's fault it didn't work out that way.

"Gianni!" he burst out. "Can you finally answer my question! Is it true you've got a girlfriend?"

And Ella joined in: "Tell the truth, Gianni! You only need to say yes or no."

But Gianni said nothing at all. Not until Grandma gave him a reproachful look.

"Well, it's like this…" he said tentatively. "I have met someone I think Dani is going to like very much… May I introduce you to Sadie?"

Dani's eyes flew wide open. This was Sadie!

Sadie smiled at Dani, but Dani didn't smile back.

"Won't you say hello?" asked Dad.

Dani shook her head.

Sadie went red in the face and started looking for something in her handbag—a packet of cigarettes.

Ella wrinkled her nose.

"It's bad for your health to smoke," she announced. "You should know that, working in a hospital."

Sadie quickly put the packet back in her bag.

Ella looked at her critically and turned to Dani's father.

"In any case, I think you should have talked to your daughter first," she said.

"Why should he?" asked Sven. "Is there something wrong with Sadie?"

"See for yourself!" said Ella. "She smokes!"

"Only when I'm nervous," mumbled Sadie.

Then Grandma stepped in: "You must excuse us, Sadie, but this is a little unexpected for Dani. Since her mother died she's lived alone with her father. She's used to being everything to him…"

"Sadie knows that," Gianni interrupted, and reached for Dani again, but she wriggled away. "Please, Dani, can't you just say hello?"

Dani pressed her lips together.

"Gianni! It doesn't matter what you say," explained Ella. "Dani will never say hello to Sadie if she doesn't want to! And I understand her!"

"Ella, will you calm down," her mother said.

"No, I can't!" replied Ella. "Now Dani's whole life has been ruined! It's a catastrophe!"

"Was it a catastrophe for you when I met Paddy?" asked her mother.

"That's different," said Ella.

Dani's father crumpled in his chair. Sadie mechanically stirred her spoon in the coffee cup.

"Won't anyone try the cake?" she asked.

"Perhaps we can save it till later," Ella's mother suggested.

But there was no later, because soon after that Dani's father decided that they should go.

"It was silly of us to come here," he said. "Really. We might as well go back to the hospital. Is that what you want us to do, Dani?"

"Yes, she does," said Ella. "Can't you see how sad she is?"

"Won't you have a look at the island first?" Paddy tried.

"No, we'll go as soon as we can get hold of a taxi boat," said Dani's dad.

He eased himself slowly out of the chair and called for one.

"It'll be here in ten minutes," he said and turned again to Dani.

"I know you refused to say hello to Sadie, but perhaps you could bring yourself to say goodbye?"

Dani's face didn't change.

Then her father lost his temper.

"I'm ashamed of you," he told her. "Do you hear me? Ashamed!"

But this was too much for Grandma.

"That's enough, Gianni," she said sharply. "You could have spared us all this!"

"What do you mean?"

"You know very well."

"Bringing Sadie with me?"

"Of course. Don't you think the child has been through enough? She almost lost her father and now you turn up with an unknown woman in tow and expect her to be pleased! I don't think Dani needs any more worry. Come, Daniela!"

That is Dani's proper name, Daniela. But it's only used when things are serious.

Grandma took her by the hand and went towards the house.

"Wait," called Sadie running after them. "We can't end like this. Can I say something?"

Dani came to a stop on the steps.

"It's all my fault," said Sadie. "I shouldn't have come, but I so badly wanted to meet you."

"And now you have," said Grandma. "You can meet her again some other time. If it's still relevant."

She disappeared inside with Dani.

Sadie blinked away a tear.

Ella went up and looked at her again.

"Children can actually be very difficult," she said.

But when she tried to go on, Paddy interrupted: "Stop. That's enough now."

And that was the last word.

The taxi boat arrived and Paddy helped Gianni back onto the motorbike and drove him to the jetty.

Once again Sadie had to run.

"She didn't laugh one single time," said Ella when they had disappeared.

"But Gianni didn't tell any funny stories either," muttered Sven. "What shall we do now? Go fishing?"

Chapter 8

They went off to the fishing spot. They stood and waited silently for bites. You're supposed to be quiet when you fish, otherwise you scare them away.

But Sven couldn't be quiet for long.

He tried to lighten the gloomy mood with a few jokes.

"What did the baker do when robbers turned up?"

"Battered them," yawned Ella, because she'd read that joke on an ice cream stick.

"Who doesn't move a whisker the whole holidays?"

Ella knew that joke too, because she'd read it on another ice cream stick.

"The barber!"

Dani thought they were very bad jokes.

And then Paddy appeared.

"Come on, Sven," he said, "you can test-drive my motorboat."

Sven was overjoyed and disappeared with Ella's extra father. Dani watched them with relief.

She liked her cousin a lot, but he could be a bit dense. He didn't know how it felt for her not to be everything to her dad.

It was probably because Sven didn't have a father himself. Only a mother and a grandmother and grandfather. And a parakeet called Tiger.

Chapter 9

Only when Grandma and Sven had gone back to town did Dani start speaking again.

They were sitting on the jetty, watching the sunset.

There, right on the edge of the jetty, Dani said something no one had ever heard her say before:

"I wish I had my mother," she said.

And it was like a shiver running over the water.

"I want to be everything to somebody," she explained. "Do you know what I mean, Ella?"

"But you are!" said Ella. "You are everything to me. Write it down in your book! It should say I AM EVERYTHING TO ELLA!"

She meant the book that Dani wrote in her first year at school, called *My Happy Life*.

But that year was finished and Dani wasn't sure that her life was actually happy any more.

Besides, she no longer had the book. She had given it to her teacher at the end-of-year party.

Ella hugged Dani.

But it didn't help for long.

As soon as Ella let go Dani felt unhappy again.

"This is no good," said Ella. "I think I'll have to make a spell!"

"A spell?"

"Stay here!"

She disappeared up to the house.

When she came back she had a crow's feather and a jar of muck.

"Open your mouth and close your eyes!" she commanded.

Dani hesitated.

"Do I have to?"

"Yes, if you want to feel happy again," said Ella.

Dani did as she was told and Ella began to feed her with the muck.

First it tasted strange, but then it tasted of oats. Then it tasted of butter and cucumber.

And raisins!

When the contents of the jar were finished Dani was allowed to open her eyes.

Ella was dancing about with catlike steps, humming a single note and waving the crow's feather.

She moved faster and faster, and in a minute she pulled Dani up and made her join the dance.

Just as Dani was starting to find it funny, Ella suddenly stopped and let out a loud, blood-curdling cry.

"There!" she gasped. "Now your father doesn't have a girlfriend any more!"

She had hardly uttered the words when the door opened up at the house and Ella's mother waved the phone.

"Dani," she called. "Telephone for you!"

Dani ran so fast she almost flew.

Chapter 10

It was Dad!

"Dani, I can't sleep," he said. "I'm so terribly sorry!"

"Me too," whispered Dani.

"Everything went wrong today. It didn't turn out at all as I thought it would."

"I know," said Dani.

"But you can sleep better tonight. I've talked to Sadie…"

Dad cleared his throat and Dani pressed the phone harder to her ear.

"I've told her that it's just too soon for me to have a new relationship."

"Rela...what?"

"Too soon to have...a girlfriend, I mean. I'll never do anything you're not happy with! The main thing is that you're happy again... Can you hear me, Dani? Are you there?"

"Yes, the main thing is that I'm happy again," Dani repeated.

And so it was. The main thing was that she would be happy again.

Dad paused for a moment. Then he said: "Of course Sadie is sad..."

"She can probably find someone else to be a girlfriend to," suggested Dani.

"I'm sure she can," Dad agreed. "But she'd thought up lots of fun things you could do together while I still have to be in the hospital."

"Like what?"

"Like a little trip to her sister Lisette who has Iceland ponies."

"In Iceland?"

"No, in Risinge."

"Is that close to Iceland?" asked Dani.

"No, it's close to Northbrook."

"Oh, Northbrook," Dani exclaimed.

Ella lives in Northbrook when she isn't on the island.

"You could choose for yourself which horse you wanted to ride," Dad continued.

"I'm scared of horses," Dani reminded him.

"I know, but Iceland ponies are very nice and gentle."

"Ella says that too," said Dani. "Wait, Dad!"

She turned to Ella, who had followed her and was sitting close by.

"Do you want to ride Iceland ponies?" Dani asked. "Except not in Iceland."

"Where then?"

"Close to Northbrook!"

Ella nodded eagerly.

"That's all right," Dani said to her dad. "But only if Ella can come too."

"I'm sure that will be fine," said Dad. "Sadie will do anything to be able to meet you again!"

"It's fine for her to meet *me*," said Dani. "Just not *you*!"

"I'll tell her that," Dad promised.

"Don't forget, Ella has to be allowed to choose her own horse too!"

"Absolutely. What do you think about next weekend? Sadie could come and get you."

Ella nodded even more eagerly.

"Yes," said Dani, "but tell Sadie that Ella is just as nice as me. In fact, nicer even!"

"Yes, I know…"

Dad cleared his throat again.

"Then maybe Sadie could come and visit us sometime," he suggested carefully. "When I'm better, I mean."

"In that case she could only meet me," said Dani.

"Where would I go then?"

"You can go and see Grandma and Grandpa and help Sven with his homework."

"Or go in the garage," whispered Ella.

"Or be in the kitchen making dinner," suggested Dad. "And now we'll say goodnight!"

The phone call ended and Ella tickled Dani on the nose with the crow's feather.

"It worked," she said happily.

"What did?" asked Dani.

"The spell!"

Chapter 11

And so the day came to an end.

By the time Dani and her father had finished talking, the sky was black and stars were peeping out.

As they watched, one suddenly broke loose and hurtled through the sky.

"Look!" cried Ella. "We have to wish for something! What do you wish for?"

Dani didn't have to think for long. She always had a couple or three or four wishes stored up.

"I wish that we're allowed to take our hamsters to school when it starts next year. And you?"

"Me?" said Ella. "I don't know. When you're here I have everything I could wish for."

And a familiar feeling spread through Dani.

She felt warm and light inside even though it was so dark around them. Happiness had turned up again!

In that moment life was exactly as it should be.

Life according to Dani.

This edition first published in 2016 by Gecko Press
PO Box 9335, Marion Square, Wellington 6141, New Zealand
info@geckopress.com

English language edition © Gecko Press Ltd 2016

First published by Bonnier Carlsen, Stockholm, Sweden

Published in the English language by arrangement with Bonnier Group Agency,
Stockholm, Sweden
Original title: *Livet enligt Dunne*
Text © Rose Lagercrantz 2015
Illustrations © Eva Eriksson 2015

The cost of this translation was defrayed by a subsidy from the Swedish
Arts Council, gratefully acknowledged.

Distributed in the United States and Canada by Lerner Publishing Group, www.lernerbooks.com
Distributed in the United Kingdom by Bounce Sales and Marketing, www.bouncemarketing.co.uk
Distributed in Australia by Scholastic Australia, www.scholastic.com.au
Distributed in New Zealand by Upstart Distribution, www.upstartpress.co.nz

Translated by Julia Marshall
Edited by Penelope Todd
Typesetting by Vida & Luke Kelly, New Zealand
Printed in China by Everbest Printing Co. Ltd, an accredited ISO 14001 & FSC certified printer

Hardback (USA) ISBN: 978-1-776570-70-6
Paperback ISBN: 978-1-776570-71-3
Ebook available

For more curiously good books, visit www.geckopress.com